THIS LITTLE TIGER BOOK BELONGS TO:

LITTLE TIGER PRESS
An imprint of Magi Publications
22 Manchester Street, London W1M 5PG
This paperback edition published 1998
First published in Great Britain 1998
Text © 1998 A.H.Benjamin
Illustrations © 1998 Tim Warnes
A.H.Benjamin and Tim Warnes have asserted
their rights to be identified as the author and
illustrator of this work under the Copyright,
Designs and Patents Act, 1988.
Printed in Belgium by Proost NV, Turnhout
ISBN 1 85430 446 1
3 5 7 9 10 8 6 4

For Sue and Paul
A.H.B.
For Jess
T.W.

IT COULD HAVE BEEN WORSE...

by A.H.Benjamin

illustrated by Tim Warnes

Mouse was on his way back home after visiting his town cousin, when . . . .

He lost his balance
and fell to the ground.

WHOOPS!

WHOOM

"Ouch!" said Mouse.
"This isn't my
lucky day."

But it could have
been worse!

Mouse picked himself up
and carried on his way.
He came to an open field
and was scurrying across it,
when . . . .

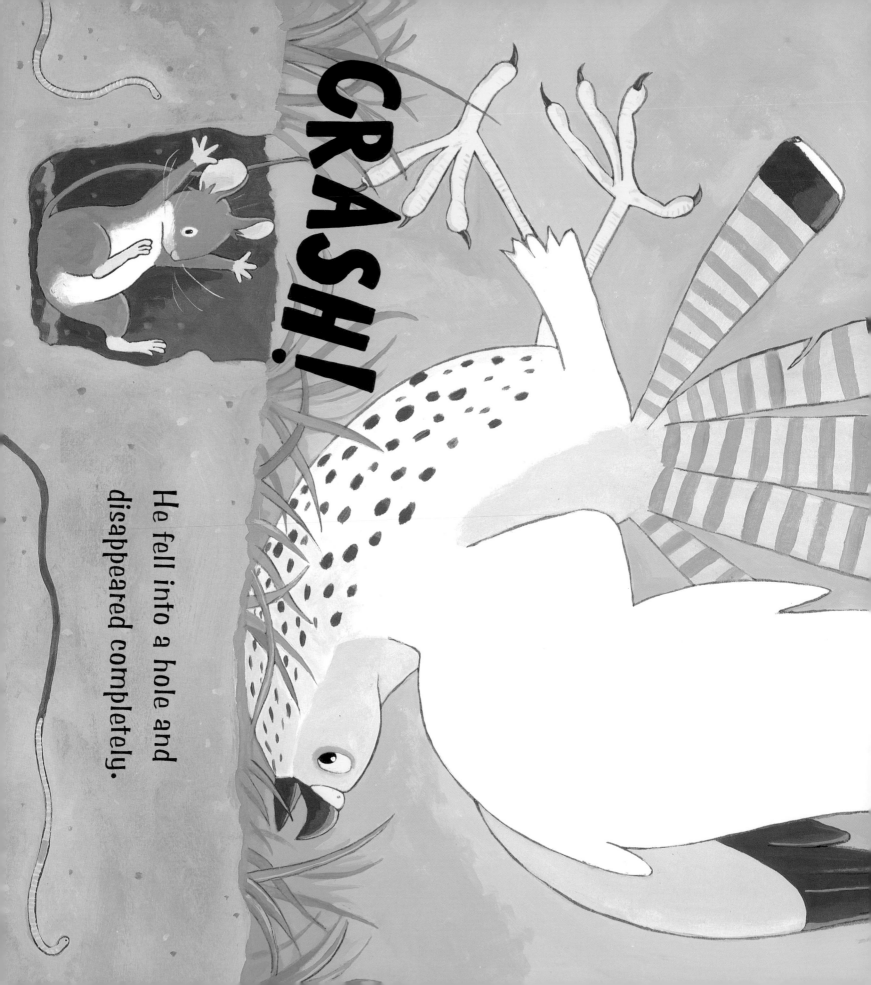

CRASH!

He fell into a hole and disappeared completely.

"Why do things *always* go wrong for me?" grumbled Mouse.

But it could have been worse!

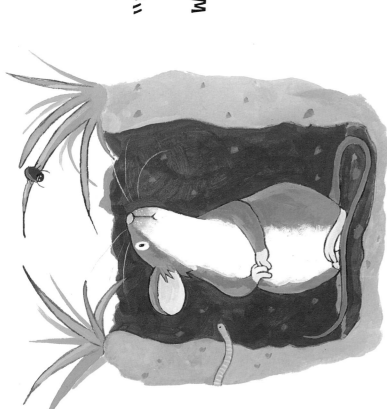

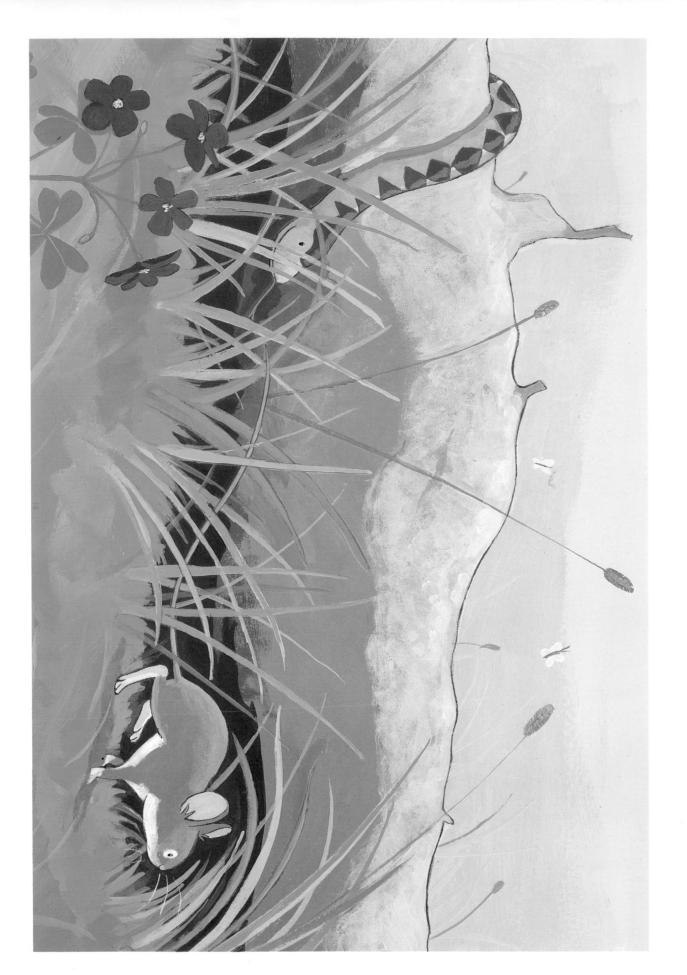

Mouse clambered out of the hole
and was off again.

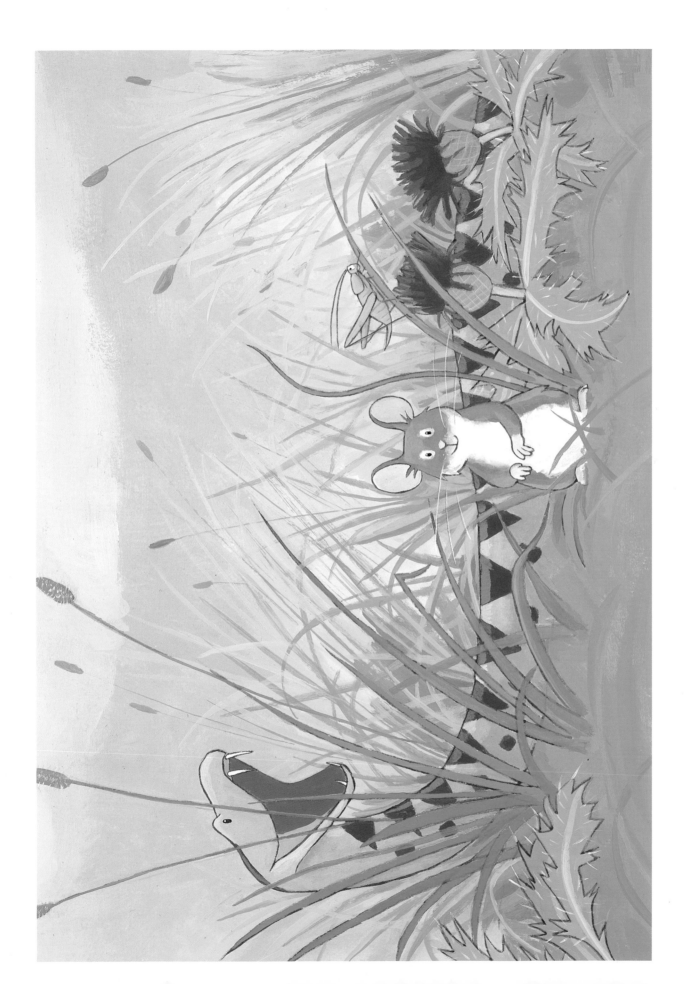

"I think I'll take a rest," he said.

Mouse had just found a nice comfy spot,

when . . . .

OUCH!

He sat on a thistle and
shot into the air.

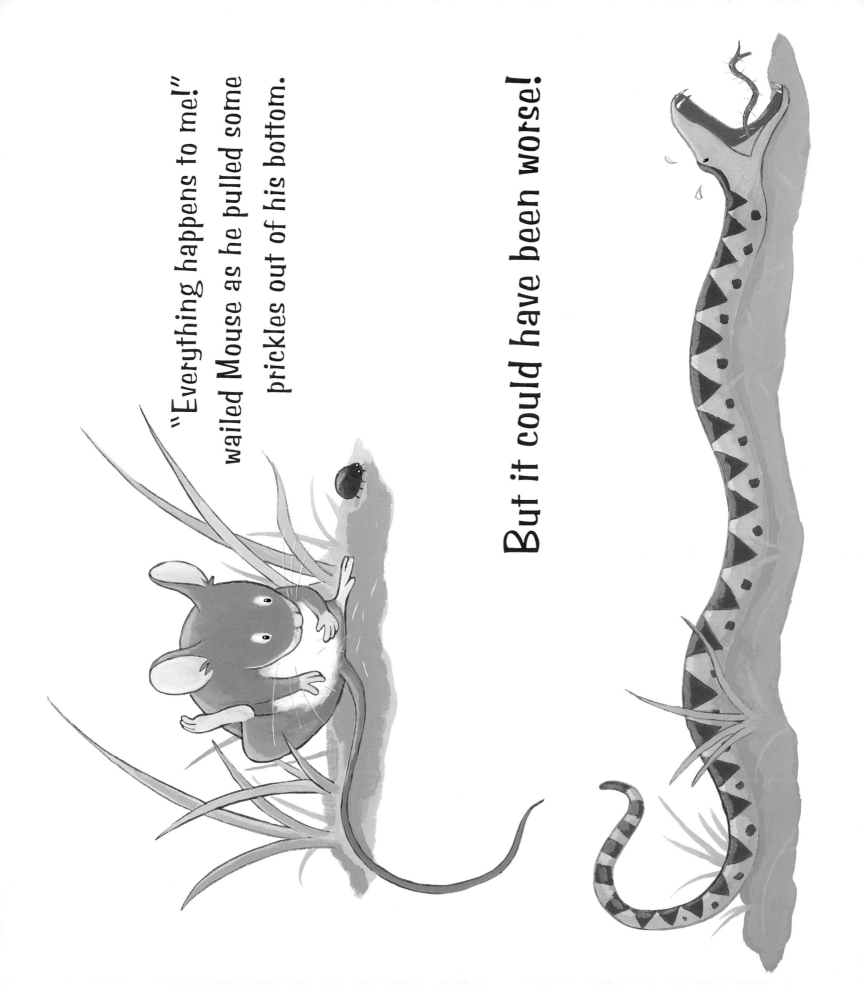

"Everything happens to me!" wailed Mouse as he pulled some prickles out of his bottom.

But it could have been worse!

Mouse walked down the hill
until he reached a stream.
He began to cross it
by the stepping stones,
when . . . .

SPLASH!

He landed
in the water.

"I'll catch my death of cold!"
complained Mouse.

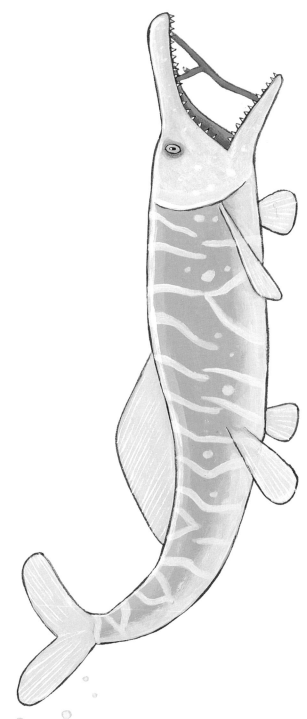

But it could have been worse!

Mouse paddled to the edge of the stream
and climbed out of the water.

Shaking himself dry, he was just about to scramble down a steep bank, when . . . .

He lost his footing and
skidded right to the bottom.

WHEEE!

"I'll be black and blue all over," cried Mouse.

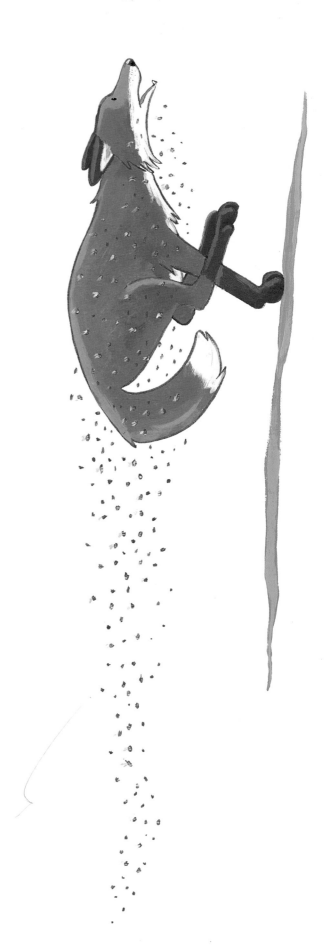

But it could have been worse!

Mouse staggered to his feet
and ran all the way home.

"It's been a terrible day," he said to his mum as she bathed his cuts and bruises. "I fell in a hole, got wet in the river and —"

"Never mind, son," said Mum . . . .

"It could have been *much* worse!"

Join the LITTLE TIGER CLUB now for lots more books to enjoy!

Schools can join too and will receive a special enrolment pack.

Join the LITTLE TIGER CLUB now and receive a special Little Tiger goody bag containing badges, pencils and more! Once you become a member you will receive details of special offers, competitions and news of new books. Why not write a book review? The best reviews received will be published on book covers or in the Little Tiger catalogue.

I don't want to go to bed!
Julie Sykes
Tim Warnes

Smudge
Julie Sykes
and
Jane Chapman

Ridiculous!
by Michael Coleman
Illustrated by Gwyneth Williamson

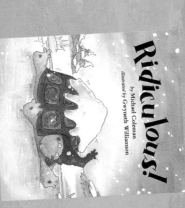

DORA'S EGGS
by Julie Sykes
Pictures by Jane Chapman

The LITTLE TIGER CLUB is free to join. Members can cancel their membership at any time, and are under no obligation to purchase any books. If you would like details of the Little Tiger Club or a catalogue of books please contact: Little Tiger Press, 22 Manchester Street, London W1M 5PG, UK. Telephone 0171 486 0925
Visit our website at: www.littletiger.okukbooks.com

Mouse, Look Out!
Judy Waite
illustrated by Norma Burgin

Laura's Star
Klaus Baumgart

MARK EZRA
The Prickly Hedgehog
pictures by Gavin Rowe

A.H. BENJAMIN
A DUCK SO SMALL
ELISABETH HOLSTIEN